The UNDERWEAR Book

Megan Tingley Books

LITTLE, BROWN AND COMPANY

New York   Boston

For my Dad for always making me laugh.
Love,
Todd

Little, Brown and Company • Hachette Book Group • 1290 Avenue of the Americas, New York, NY 10104
Visit our website at www.lb-kids.com

Little, Brown and Company is a division of Hachette Book Group, Inc.
The Little, Brown name and logo are trademarks of Hachette Book Group, Inc.

The publisher is not responsible for websites (or their content) that are not owned by the publisher.

First Edition: August 2012
Originally published in hardcover by Little, Brown and Company as *Underwear Do's and Don'ts*

Library of Congress Cataloging-in-Publication Data

Parr, Todd.
[Underwear do's and don'ts]
The underwear book / Todd Parr.—1st pbk. ed.
p. cm.
"Megan Tingley books."
ISBN 978-0-316-18831-9
1. Underwear—Humor. I. Title.
PN6231.U52P37 2012
818'.602—dc23
2011027355

10 9 8 7 6 5 4

IM

Printed in China

There are many underwear do's and don'ts.

Have lots of different kinds of underwear

Don't

Wear
it all
at
once

Wash your underwear

Don't

Use too much soap

Put your clean underwear away

Put it in the freezer

Go shopping for underwear with a hippo

Don't

Let her try it on

RRIP

DO

Wear new underwear on the first day of school

Don't

Bring it for
show-and-tell

Do

Dress up your dog in underwear

Don't

Use your sister's favorite pair

DO

Wear fancy underwear under your dress

Don't

Hang upside down on the monkey bars

Do

Give cool underwear
as a present

Go swimming in your underwear

Don't

Jump off the diving board

DO

Wear
polka-dot
underwear
to a
party

Don't

Wear a plain pair

Do

Wear striped underwear if you're a zebra

Don't

Wear
polka-dotted
ones

Do

Bring extra underwear
when you go fishing

Don't

Use it as bait

No matter what underwear you wear, always feel good about yourself!

Love, ♥
ToDD